T.M. Cooks is the pen name of the following collaborative writing team. The contributors are;

- Freya Boyd

- Tiegan Cross

- Elizabeth Fairclough

- Emily Marsh

- Nieve Owens

- Euan Sandiford

- Nicholas Smith

- Nieve Smith

with cover design by Laura Bunyan. The project was overseen by Adam Steiner and Laura Bunyan.

The group cheerfully acknowledges the wonderful help given by:

- Mr Lovelady

- Mrs Worrall

- Mrs Twist

- Miss Barker

- Miss Fairfax

- Mr Wright

- Mrs Sherman - For allowing the project to take place.

- Laura Bunyan

- Adam Steiner

It's been a wonderful opportunity, and everyone involved has been filled with incredible knowledge and enthusiasm.

Finally, we would like to thank all staff at The Sutton Academy for their support in releasing our novelists from lessons for a full week. This project has been supported by SHINE.

The group started to plan out their novel at 8.50 on Monday 13 November 2017 and completed their last proofreading at 14.40 on Friday 17th November 2017.

We are incredibly proud to state that every word of the story, every idea, every chapter and yes, every mistake, is entirely their own work. No teachers, parents or other students touched a single key during this process, and we would ask readers to keep this in mind.

We are sure you will agree that this is an incredible achievement. It has been a true delight and privilege to see this group of young people turn into professional novelists in front of our very eyes. We hope you enjoy our book.

The Invasion Of Planet X

T. M. Cooks

Contents

3

Chapter 1

The End Is The Beginning

Location:Scotland,   United Kingdom

Time: 14:45,   2077

Tony was walking home from school as

he usually did on a Friday evening. He wasn't in a very good mood seeing as his bag was stolen by the school bullies, Finley and Ben, and then he was given a detention for something he didn't even do. Tony was livid. He sat on a bench that overlooked the lake, well if you could even call it a lake, it was more of a pond, so he could calm down. He watched the graceful swans glide across the water and the sunlight dance on the lakes. He sat still. The wind blew through his hair and the trees swayed peacefully. He looked down at the water. "What is my purpose?" Tony thought as he glared at his reflection that sat on the water's surface. As he continued to gaze at his reflection, he saw a bright red light glowing on the rippling water. Tony looked up to see a burning inferno falling from the sky and he realised, it was a bomb, and it was about to blow.

The sound of terror filled the air and the thought of his family being obliterated filled his heart with dread. Sirens bleeped in every direction and screams of fear hung in the air. Tony's heart pounded and it was jumping out of his chest. He sprinted out of the park, jumping over bins, that had been knocked over by the stampede of people, and sliding on the hoods of parked cars. When he got to the main road a flood of people rushed past him like flowing water. Panic filled his head as he worried that he wouldn't be able to reach his family. He had to get his family. Tony ploughed through the crowd and rushed across the street and he continued to sprint home.

Tony burst through the front door of

his home.

"Mum, where are you?" Tony yelled as he rushed up the stairs.

"Tony, we're up here!" Tony's parents screamed.

Tony entered his parents room to see them packing their bags and to see his sister, Poppie, cramming all of her clothes and belongings into her suitcase.

"Tony, thank god you are okay, " Tony's mum sobbed as she held him close to her.

"I am so happy you're here, I would hate to leave you behind, " Poppie said as she embraced him.

"Why are you all packing?" Tony asked as he sat on his parents bed.

"Tony, we have been told to evacuate earth, " Tony's mum said as she picked up her suitcase.

"What do you mean we have to leave earth?" Tony asked.

"We have been told by the police to get to an evacuation pod as soon as possible, " Tony's mother added "We have to leave before the bomb drops because when it drops, it is predicted that it will destroy the whole of Europe and the waste from the bomb will kill all life on earth, ". Tony froze in fear. His heart sank to the bottom of his chest. He sat knowing that his home would be destroyed in just a few hours and that his whole planet would just be a ball of despair filled with lost hopes and dreams that drifts through space slowly decaying.

Tony had packed his bags and he and his family got their cases and put them in the back of their red Mini. Tony and his family got in the car. The car was filled with silence, the only sound in the car was the sound of a humming engine. Tony stared out of the window. He watched the huddles of families sobbing on the side of the road as the car passed them and he looked at the rampaging streets filled with people fighting for their lives. A tear rolled down Tony's face.

Chapter 2

Evacuate

Tony and his family reached an evacuation pod and they got out of the car. Outside of the pod hundreds of people where stood fighting to get into the pod. Tony grabbed his case and he and his family walked up to the guard stood prominently in front of the pod. Tony approached the man. The man looked at Tony and his family, nodded, and then let them pass. Tony stepped into the pod. The pod was clean and extremely sleek, it had a white casing and the windows were blacked out. Tony sat on the white leather seats and he strapped himself in. The metal door beeped and it slid shut. The shuttle was cramped as each shuttle had to hold at least 10000 people and there was around 12000 people in ours.

Tony gazed out of the blacked out window. He could see his friends from school stood outside of the pod trying to push through the guard. He even saw the school bullies, Finley and Ben, crying outside of the pod. Tony then realised how lucky he was and that not everyone would survive.

Tony sat and wondered what was going to happen to him and what was going to happen to the people outside. He wondered if the people outside were going to die, or if he was going to die. Tony began to panic and his heart began to race. All of these questions were running around in his head. "Am I going to die? What's going to happen? Are they going to die? Is this the end?" Tony said out loud and then it happened.

The bomb had exploded, heat radiated across the city and the sky went red with fire. The sound of screaming filled the silence that was once in the pod and terror spread across the city. A shockwave penetrated the city destroying the tops of buildings and obliterating the cars on the road. The shrieks of the crowd outside could be heard as they began to bang on the side of the pod in anger.

Red lights flashed left, right and centre, the pod began to beep and it shook violently.An automated voice announced on the speaker "launching in 10 seconds". The pod began to shake even more violently and Tony's heart pounded like a drum. He looked out of the window to see the shockwave was about to hit. "10, 9, 8, " the voice said as the shockwave got nearer and nearer and as the pod began to shake even more violently. "7, 6, 5, 4" the voice said again Tony began to panic once more. "3, 2, 1, Launch" the voice said. Finally, the pod was shaking more violently than ever. As Tony looked outside he could see the earth slowly shrinking behind him and he could see the stars burning brightly ahead of him. He was in space he undid his belt and he felt himself become weightless but as he looked back

again once more he could see his planet
slowly fade away and he could see a black
cloud spread across the surface of the earth.

Chapter 3

The Journey

Location: Space

Time: Unknown

Tony drifted back into his seat and he strapped himself back in. He could see the glow of the flame from behind the pod and he could see the light from the stars that shimmered in the distance.Tony sat speechless as he and the rest of the passengers drifted through space. He turned to see his sister crying beside him.

"What's up?" Tony asked as he put his hand on the shoulder of his sister, Poppie.

"Our home, it's gone, " Poppie explained as she watched the earth slowly drift away. Tony didn't know how to respond so he hugged Poppie instead. Suddenly, a tall figure emerged from the cockpit and a hush fell over the passengers. The figure had blue eyes and blonde hair that shone in the starlight and he was wearing a blue outfit with golden straps.

"My name is Tom, " the figure said "I will lead you in your new life and protect you on your new home, Planet X".

A hologram appeared in front of the figure, and the hologram was showing a pale green planet with turquoise waters and purple skies.

"That is your new home, " Tom said as he pointed to the hologram. The hologram disappeared and Tom went back to the cockpit. The passengers began to chatter.

Tony was excited to see his new planet but he was also filled with fear. He sat wondering what life would be like on this new planet and wondered what creatures would also live there. In the corner of Tony's eye he could see a strange object that was stagnant in space. It was swirling in a hypnotic way and it looked as if it was a hole in space and as if a piece of space had been erased from existence. Tony noticed that the pod was turning around and was going at full speed, heading right for the swirling hole.

The ship was getting closer and closer to the hole. Tony then felt a strong force pulling him towards the hole and passengers looked around confused. The pod was being sucked into the hole and Tony could hear a peculiar humming sound. As the pod drifted closer to the hole the humming sound stopped. Silence. Suddenly, the pod was stretched and warped and Tony's body began to stretch as well as the rest of the passengers.

"What's happening?" A passenger yelled as she looked down at her legs to see them being stretched.

All of the passengers who were in the pod began screaming in terror as they saw their limbs being stretched, then the stretching stopped. Rapidly, the hole engulfed the entire pod in an instant and the pod was being flooded with bright light. Tony looked out of the window in curiosity and he saw beams of light shooting past the pod and then the light faded away. Silence.

Tony looked around frantically to see where he was. He saw that the once empty space that he and the rest of the passengers drifted through had now been replaced with colour and wonder. Tony turned to Poppie.

"Where are we?" Tony asked as he continued to gaze at the array of colours that surrounded him.

"I don't know?" Poppie said as she turned to the window in amazement. Tom

23

came out of the cockpit again and showed
Tony and the rest of the passengers a new
hologram.

"Welcome to galaxy C632, " Tom said
as he pointed to an area on his hologram.
He enlarged the hologram to reveal a shimmering burst of colour and light and the
passengers sat speechless. "Our new galaxy
is amazing, " Tony yelled in excitement.
As Tony looked at the colour filled galaxy
he saw another ship but it looked different
to any ship he had seen before.

"Whose ship is that, " Tony asked as he
turned back round, but no one answered.

Tony continued to gaze outside of the
shuttle, wondering who the ship belonged
to and where it come from. He sat silent.
He continued to watch the stars pass by
the window when he saw a planet getting

closer and closer.

"Is this our new home, " Tony asked himself as he pressed his face up against the window. The planet was huge much bigger than Earth and even bigger than Jupiter and the surface of it was of a pale green colouration and the planet was wrapped in a blanket of pale yellow clouds.

The pod began to slow down as it approached the planet. The pod had ripped through the atmosphere of the planet and Tony was sat anxiously thinking of his new home but on the inside he was bubbling with excitement. He sat restlessly. The pod had gotten closer and closer to the ground and was about to land on the pale green surface of the planet. Tony was about to explode with excitement and he was desperate to get out of the cramped pod that he had been sat in for 3 hours. The pod halted to a stop. Tom had come back out of the cockpit,

"Welcome to Planet X, you're new home forever, " Tom said as he opened the door to the pod. Everyone in the pod began to chatter in excitement.

"Are you ready to take your first step on your new planet, " Tom said as he smiled at Tony.

Chapter 4

Planet X

Location:Planet X

Time: Unknown

Rapidly, Tony ripped his belt off and dashed outside of the pod and he stood speechless. He rubbed his eyes in disbelief.

Tony and the rest of the passengers stood shocked as they looked out across the new planet. Bright yellow clouds glided through the air and the pale green grass covered the soft brown soil like a blanket. The planet was paradise, it was magical, it was amazing.

Tony sprinted outside and dashed around like an excited child. He wanted to explore and see everything there is to see.

"Hold on Tony!" Poppie yelled as she grabbed Tony by the wrist.

"We don't want to lose you, or do we?" Poppie laughed as she pushed Tony.

"Shut up, " Tony said as he pushed Poppie back in a playful way.

Tom stepped outside and gave everyone a map that showed them where the city was.

"There is a map, it will show you where to find the city, " Tom pointed to an area on the map and a flashing red dot appeared on it. "That is where the city is, feel free to explore your new home, but don't go in these areas as they are highly restricted, " Tom explained as he tapped on the map and highlighted the restricted areas with a red "X".

Then Tom disappeared into the pod and it took off.

"Ready to go and explore?" Tony asked as he opened his map.

"Well we will have to and ask Mum and Dad and if I say that you can't go somewhere, you don't go there, ok? " Poppie looked at her and Tony's parents and grinned. Poppie is a very protective person seeing as she is a soldier who has to disguise herself as a man and she has seen many of her friends die.

"Go on then, " Tony and Poppie's Mum said as she smiled at them with glee.

Tony and Poppie sprinted away to go and explore. Tony looked up at the sky and to his surprise it wasn't blue but it was a beautiful lavender colour with the yellow clouds than intermingled and two suns hovered above the clouds. The trees had hanging bulbs that glowed a warm yellow colour and the trees had hexagonal fruit that shimmered in the sunlight. A huge orange rock stood prominently in the center of a field that was filled with massive stalks, covered in bean like fruits. Suddenly, Tony heard a strange noise coming from behind the rock.

"What was that?" Tony said as he hid

behind Poppie.

"Don't be such an baby, " Poppie giggled. Cautiously, Poppie began to approach the direction the noise was coming from. When she reached the rock she could see a small creature shaking behind a bush. The creature had short stumpy legs and was covered in blue hair. It had yellow and orange striped horns and it was about the size of a small dog.

"Come on Tony it's harmless, " Poppie explained as she picked it up and began to stroke it. Tony began to pat it's head and the creature began to make a soft gurgling noise. Tony smiled at it.

"It's kinda cute, " Tony said as he hugged the creature.

"Well, we should he

ad back before Mum and Dad start to

worry, we can always explore tomorrow, "
Poppie said as she put the creature back
behind the rock and began to walk back
to the city.

Tony and Poppie began to approach the
city that had been built years before they
had landed. The city was spectacular. A
huge sign stood proudly and on the sign
was "Indigo City" written in bold purple
letters. A purple force field protected the
city like a shield. The city was filled with
immaculate buildings that were sleek and
pristine and rail with a silver train wrapped
around the city like a ribbon on a present.
In the center of the city was the leaders
tower, which was a grand tower that stood
watching over the city. The tower had a
purple beacon that shone out of the top
and a purple glow radiated across the city.

The tower was magnificent with it's white covered walls and it's blue stained windows. The air of the city smelt fresh and clean and the sound of chatter filled the air. Tony and Poppie could see their parents waving at them as they sat on a bench that looked out across the city. Tony and Poppy dashed over to them to tell them about what they saw.

As Poppie told Tony and her parents about what they saw Tony looked up into the sky thinking about what had seen on Earth. Tony would never forget what happened on Earth. He continued to look up at the purple sky and he stared at the bright suns as he wondered what had happened to the people left there. The sun's glowed like a light and the sky was clear. Suddenly, a strange object blocked out all

33

of the sun's light. It was the ship Tony saw in space.

The ship began to hover over the city blocking out all of the light from the sun's. The ship surrounded the city like a vulture waiting to eat it's prey and a whirring noise echoed through the streets. The city went dark. Suddenly, hundreds of military trucks zoomed past the bench Tony and his family were sat on. The trucks rushed outside of the city and thousands of soldiers flooded out of them. The sound of yelling filled the air as the soldiers aimed all of their weapons at the ship and Tom ordering the troops to prepare to fire. They were scared.

The ship began to lower and the whirring sound began to get softer. The soldiers were now preparing to shoot. The ship stopped and it had landed. All of the soldiers surrounded the ship, they were going to attack. Then, a door on the ship began to slide open and an silhouette of an creature stood in the doorway.

Chapter 5

The Aliens Visit

Location:Planet X

Time: Unknown

L.U.N.A looked at the bizarre creatures that were standing in front of her and her own species and wondered what they were doing on their land. The peculiar creatures looked somewhat confused and frightened, did they know where they were? Why were they here? "They shouldn't be here, they must leave immediately, "L.U.N.A said, and she intended to make sure they did. This world was extremely dangerous, not to mention the leader of L.U.N.A's kind was known to be cruel and power hungry. If the leader would eliminate one of his own kind without hesitation she did not desire to think what he would do to an unknown species. If these creatures attempted to attack them they would suffer but it wouldn't be L.U.N.A's doing, they would die by her leaders hands.

One of the servants stepped forward while the rest of her kind stood back, it seems her leader was trying to offer peace to the unknown species. This was an unusual approach normally he would order the guards to attack them and show no mercy, the alien leader was brutal and usually didn't listen to his kind. Why was he trying to offer peace to these creatures peace? It didn't make sense for him to want peace between L.U.N.A's kind, he was up to something and she didn't wish to take part in whatever evil scheme he had concocted. He was probably planning to use them for his own gain. L.U.N.A's leader was the most selfish of all of her kind, that was one of the things that she didn't admire about him. He would never think about anyone else but himself.

The look of terror didn't leave the faces of the strange species, L.U.N.A noticed one of them was deep in thought he didn't seem to be scared like the rest of his kind. If he was not scared what could he have been feeling? He was just confronted by the dominant species of the planet. L.U.N.A's species was known for being ruthless, powerful and last but definitely not least, selfish. There was no possible way that they could live in peace with another species. When their previous leaders had tried to make peace with species other than ourselves it lead to war, it always does.

After minutes of silence there was a shout and it came from none other than the man L.U.N.A had been observing for the past few minutes. It was the man that seemed to show no fear towards L.U.N.A and the rest of her kind, she understood what the look on his face was now. He was thinking what to do. He had decided to order his kind to attack the aliens, there was no doubt about it. He was their leader and he had decided to get his kind to attack. She didn't really blame him for ordering his kind to attack. It was probably her leaders backup plan if the strange creatures didn't accept the peace offering.

Chapter 6

The War Has Begun

It seemed like their leader wasn't surprised by the fact his peace offering wasn't accepted because, not long after, the alien leader ordered the alien troops and L.U.N.A. to fight. Despite the order she stood back the peace offering wasn't her idea and it wasn't her fault that the unknown species had attacked them. "I will not fight unless things get out of hand and I want to see what my leader is planning before I fight on his behalf. I am not foolish like the rest of my kind, I don't blindly follow my leader's orders without knowing the truth first. I have my reasons for being suspicious especially because even though I am second in command my leader refuses to tell me about what he is planning." thought L.U.N.A. - who would be punished more severely than other aliens as she was the alien leaders second in command.

From the way the leader of the confusing creatures ordered his kind to attack she could tell he thought the aliens intended to kill them. However the truth is L.U.N.A.

44

didn't even know what her leader intends to do and if she didn't find out she would have disobey all of the orders her leader would give out. She wasn't like the rest of her kind, unlike the rest of them she believed trust is earned not given and her leader has not earned any of her trust. Her leader doesn't deserve trust from anyone he has done nothing but lie to L.U.N.A. and the other aliens, yet she was sure most of her kind were too scared to disobey their leader.

After a while all of the humans were fighting while she stood behind her kind thinking about the situation at hand. It was not only her who was not fighting her leader, A.L. was standing on the side lines.

"You must be proud of yourself" L.U.N.A said confidently with the new found hatred she had for my leader.

"Proud, well of course it's not every-day that you have the honour of starting a war" he replied while smirking in victory.

"I see" was all L.U.N.A said in return as she continued watching the battle that was in front of her.

The battle was halted all of a sudden by the leader of the creatures of which L.U.N.A. was now informed were called humans. It seems like the humans had relied on their leader to save them from the battle that was becoming even more deadly as she just watched. To be honest she was glad that the human leader stepped in when he did or she would have had to stop the battle herself and that wasn't something that she particularly wanted to do. However what she heard next didn't make her relieved but even more worried. The human leader wanted to go to war and it didn't help that A.L. encouraged it. So this is what his intention was, he wanted to start a war.

She should have known this was going to happen it has happened before and what makes it even worse is that she didn't do anything to try to stop it. It shouldn't be her responsibility to stop her own kind from going to war. She can't do anything about it because her leader wants to go to war and most of her kind follow his orders no matter what. She knew for a fact that some of her kind will not want to go to war but highly doubted anyone will have the guts to form a rebellion against the alien leader.

Chapter 7

The Observation

Location:Planet X

Time:Unknown

Tony looked around in amazement, baf-
fled by the atmosphere he was in. He couldn't
believe that this was the planet he was

going to be living on from now on. He even thought that it might be better than Earth, due to the fact that he now had new areas to explore and new things to discover.

Before he even knew what he was doing, Tony had wandered into areas deemed unsafe by his sister Poppie, but he didn't realise this just yet. He was in his own world thinking about the things he could do now on this completely new planet. He could still hear the chattering of people back at the city and their tones of voiced implied they were thinking the same thing he was. It made him glad that they had landed here because who knows, if they had kept traveling they might have landed somewhere no way near as beautiful.

As Tony continued to walk and explore,

picking things up from the ground and inspecting them every now and then, he heard the sounds of chattering die down slowly. Tony started feeling unsafe now that the reassuring sounds of excitable talk were no longer there. He stopped in his tracks, straining to hear anything.

"Should I go back to the city?" Tony said aloud, looking behind him. He didn't realise just how far he had walked and, in a moment of horror, he realised he had walked into highly restricted areas. Tony felt instant dread, not wondering now what he would be able to do on this new planet but now wondering what he could possibly encounter. His mind fueled this terror with instant horrific thoughts about what could be waiting for him in the walk back to base.

Tony slowly started to slope back towards the city, occasionally looking back to the all of the unlooked land that he wasn't able to adventure yet. What if someone beat him to it? He wanted to be the first one to adventure that land. He wanted to claim it for himself, he didn't want anyone else to have it.

As Tony was walking back, he heard loud yet distant screams. He identified a mixture of emotions that came with the screams. Screams of terror, sorrow and what sounded like a type of battle screech. Tony started walking quicker, slowing down and then speeding up again, not knowing if he wanted to know the situation that was taking place at that moment in time.

"I hope everything and everyone is alright..." Tony said aloud as he started to run towards the meeting point.

Tony reached the meeting point and, to his horror yet also interest, he saw a species of which he had never once encountered.

"What are they?" Tony thought as he looked at them in wonder, a few people running past him as he did so. Tony stood there, staring at them in awe as more and more people ran away. Tony didn't understand why people were running away from them.

They seemed calm enough until...the humans started attacking. All of a sudden the seemingly calm aliens charged and started to do everything they could to prevent the humans hurting them. They were fighting violence with violence which, in Tony's opinion, didn't work properly. His awe quickly turned into horror as he watched people he loved and friends from childhood run and scream and sometimes get attacked.

Tony felt traumatized by what he was seeing, feeling like he would never be able to forget the faces of terror that seemed to be running towards him but always ran past him. Tony was frozen in place, unable to move in the crowd that was running in the direction of which he had just came back from. Within minutes of the fight, Tony was being pushed backwards by the current of people and his vision was blurred. Tony had no control of where he wanted to go. He eventually gave up struggling and just let it happen, thinking of the traumatized faces of the people he loved.

Chapter 8

The Second Movement

Location:Planet X

Time:Unknown

"Okay everyone, please remain calm!"

Poppie, the female soldier, shouted as she tried to gather all of the younger children together and keep them protected.

"Everyone follow me immediately! We need to find safety quickly!" she called, a look of intense panic on her face as she ran in the opposite direction to what would be considered a new battlefield. All of the younger children were crying for their parents of whom probably sacrificed themselves for their children.

The older children, presumably teenagers, were doing all they could to help. Rounding up the younger children and conducting head counts, the teenagers were just as panicked and wondering what was happening.

As if by magic, Tony felt a rush of adrenaline and he started helping round people up.

Poppie looked at him and gave him a quick smile of gratitude. Poppie and Tony had been close since Tony was a baby, and being brother and sister brought them closer together. The time they spent together now was special due to the fact that they had been separated for five years when Tony was ten years old. It was probably the hardest five years that Tony had ever lived through. The years had been dull without his sister, but she was back now and that was what really mattered. He would do anything now to show her just how much he had grown up in the past five years, and this was only the first thing he was going to do that to prove it.

Once everyone had been gathered, Tony took up the rear end of the crowd making sure that no one fell behind. He had to pick a few children up and carry them for a moment whilst they caught their breath and gained the strength to run again. As Tony looked around him he saw the looks of pure terror on everyone's face as they too ran in the same direction of Poppie. Tony wondered what was going on in their minds and if they were thinking about the same thing as him. What was going on? Would everyone be safe? What were those things that seemingly appeared out of nowhere?

These thoughts quickly had to stop due to the fact that Tony had to pick up a young child that have tripped and fallen over. He was sobbing loudly crying for his mother, but he looked unhurt. Tony scooped the young child up in his arms, holding him close to his chest. The child looked up at him, his eyes watery.

"Where's my mum?" he cried, pummeling Tony in the chest.

"Hey little man! Stop that, " Tony said, smiling down at him "She'll be here soon, don't you worry" Tony said. He was fully aware that he had just told this child an empty promise but he didn't know what else to say to him.

"What's your name then, little man?" Tony asked whilst running fast to catch up with the group.

"Jack, " he mumbled into Tony's chest.

"What an awesome name. So Jack, do you think you can run again and show me how grown up you are?" Tony replied, trying to encourage him.

"I can try. Will you tell my mum how brave I was if i do?" Jack said.

"Sure, " Tony said, lowering the young

59

child down to the ground.

Tony watched Jack run off, feeling the guilt settle in as he thought about the false hope that he had just filled that child with.

Chapter 9

The Bunker

After what felt like years, Poppie finally slowed down. Tony heard her shouting something that sounded like "stand back" and he heard a loud crashing sounds. Panic filled him as the thoughts of what could have happened started flooding his mind. Then the crowd surged forward and he realised that they had found a safe space to stay.

It was cramped to say the least, obviously not made to be inhabited by so many people at once but it was a fascinating place to look around at.

The walls were high and made of what looked like titanium that glistened so brightly it was sometimes nearly blinding, wooden shelves surrounded them on every wall and there was a strange bulk of bizarre looking food on one of the walls. Tony inspected it closely and decided that this was not human, but belonged to whatever had attacked one they had landed. On another one of the titanium walls lay some odd looking artillery. Tony examined one of the mysterious pieces of weaponry and decided that he definitely liked these weapons more than human ones as they looked and seemed more interesting.

Tony approached Poppie of whom was conducting a head count of all the children. Once she had finished she had a look of sincere worry on her face. She turned to Tony, her voice shaking as she spoke.

"Tony...we're missing a few kids." she whispered.

She took Tony's hands in hers and whispered

"What if their parents survive on Earth somehow and when we go back they never see their children again?"

"Don't worry Poppie, I'll go and look for them" Tony said, bravery in his voice but not in his heart. He had no idea what he was saying but he wanted to help in any way possible.

"Are you crazy? It's too dangerous, I

won't let you!" Poppie shouted, clutching Tony's wrists.

He shook her off and turned towards the door. Tony heard Poppie sigh behind him.

"Fine. But if you don't come back within the hour, we'll assume the worst."

Tony looked back and nodded. He didn't say anything, he just walked out of the alien bunker and shut the door behind him. He looked around at the atmosphere and only then did he realise the situation he was in.

Tony started walking around, looking for any sign of life.

"I wonder if the other children just froze in shock back at the meeting zone?" he thought to himself. He started observing the horizon, his eyes started playing tricks on him.

After half an hour or so, Tony tripped over what he thought was a rock. He then heard what sounded like a muffled ouch' so he looked down. There, lying on the floor, was a female teenager who was lying in the fetal position.

Chapter 10

New Friends

Location: Planet X

Time:Still unknown

Tony had been looking around for about half an hour when he suddenly tripped and fell to the ground.

"Ouch!" he exclaimed. He started checking his ankle for a sprain or a break but it seemed fine. He tried to stand up but when he did a surge of sharp pain shot through his leg.

Tony sat down reluctantly, panicking about how he would get back to the bunker if he couldn't walk properly. Eventually the next half hour would pass and he would be assumed dead. He had to get back somehow, but how?

As soon as that thought crossed his mind he heard a female voice apologising over and over again.

"I'm so sorry. Sorry, so sorry, " she kept saying over and over. Tony heard her moving around, probably trying to get to her feet and possibly go over to him to help. Tony felt slightly embarrassed that he had been so careless and tripped over. He kept inspecting his ankle, refusing to look at the girl out of pure embarrassment. He eventually built up the courage to speak, mainly out of pure annoyance that this girl wouldn't stop apologising but also because he felt it would get awkward if he just stayed silent.

"Honestly, it's fine. Let's just get back to the bunker and be done with this." Tony said.

"Just help me stand up and we can get back to the bunker already." he muttered, still feeling embarrassed.

Tony went to stand up when he fell to the ground. He had forgotten about his leg and it had surprised him. For some reason, resting it had made it worse.

Tony quickly turned around, but to his

horror he saw a young girl of whom was the same specimen as the creatures he had seen at the meeting point.

"You-you're one of th-them!" he exclaimed in terror. She had started to approach him, looking like she wanted to help, but Tony felt that he couldn't trust her. Maybe if one of them were aggressive, it ran in their blood? Tony didn't know, but he wasn't just going to sit still and wait to find out.

Tony started to back up, crawling away as quick as he could whilst keeping the alien in his peripheral view. Whilst backing away, I took the time to take in her appearance. Her complexion was one of silver, shimmering beauty of which shone in the sunlight. Her vibrant pink hair loosely flowing behind her yet covering parts of her evenly proportioned face. She walked with effortless grace, a small yet noticeable bounce in her step. Her blue eyebrows were shaped to perfection and, even though it was quite the odd array of colours, her features suited her perfectly. Tony, by the time he had observed her face to the fullest, had backed away from her a considerable amount.

Tony looked at the ground around him, avoiding her eyes as to not have another moment of pure guilt. For some reason his mind was telling him to look at her, and so was his heart. He rose his head slowly but instead of seeing her looking down at him, he saw her turn around slowly and start to walk away. As Tony looked up, he saw tears in her eyes and he wished that he hadn't looked up. Guilt filled him from head to toe and he couldn't stop himself.

"I'm sorry!" Tony called out "It's just...What's your name?" he asked her without thinking.

"My-my name is..Crypton, "she replied quietly, still not turning back to face him, "what's yours?" she asked.

"I'm..Tony. I'm sorry I judged you so quickly. It was only because...well I saw your people go to attack mine and I just thought..well maybe you were the same. I had to be safe and back away." Tony explained, starting to ramble.

He immediately felt terrible about his actions, but he couldn't help what he had thought. What else was he supposed to assume once he had seen people that looks so similar to her attacking his own kind?

"Well...I guess that's okay then. I mean,

what else were you supposed to think?"
She turned around and smiled. Once again,
he had met with the beautiful face he had
closely inspected before.

"Yeah..my thoughts exactly" Tony replied,
still feeling slightly awkward.

"Might I ask you something Tony?" she
asked, pronouncing his name very slowly
and clearly as if it was difficult to say.

"Ask away, " Tony said, grinning at her.

"What do you mean by I saw your people go to attack mine'? And what exactly
are you?" Crypton asked, sounding gen-
uinely interested and confused.

So Tony explained everything. Right
from the beginning. The fact that he had
been walking home, when he saw the reflection of a bomb in the rippling water
of the lake.The fact that he had to evac-

uate his home planet, Earth and leave his friends behind.

Crypton listened intently, gasping and gaping at Tony as if he had had the most interesting life ever.

Chapter 11

The Flashback Of It All

Location: Planet X

Time: Unknown

The alien leader was as angry as a lion

roaring viciously at his servants. He looked
at me, his eyes fiery red. We must fight for
our land he declared. My heart stopped,
"Fight?" I questioned him. Why fight
when we can share the land and make peace.
"They will overpower us" he said, I saw the
rage inside of him, just waiting to come out
. "What if people died in this fight? Our
kind might die. wouldn't you think they
would rather share the land with the humans than fight and could lose their families." I said. At that moment I blocked
out all the noise and painted a picture inside of my head a picture of what it would
look like after this war. In my head I saw
families weeping while constantly looking
over at all the dead bodies. No one would
be the same. Everyone was miserable now.
The smell of decaying bodies filled the air

as families were buried their loved ones. I couldn't let this happened so I tried everything in my power to stop him from announcing war.

As I explained to him why the war wasn't a good idea, he held his fist out infront of my face and viciously pounded my face out of shape. As tears rolled down my face, I saw that my father was looking ferociously away. I knew at that moment that he wanted to take part in the war. There was an ashamed look spread across his face. Why would you want our families to be destroyed by this. What type of leader are you if you choose power over the people. I could tell that the second leader agreed with me but she never spoke up.

The leader called me a betrayer, he said that if i ever try to interfere again he will send me off the ship. I told him that i would not fight and i would persuade others not to fight. He stood up slowly and plunged over to my father. He screamed in his face and said what kind of a daughter have you raised. Tears poured down his face as he screamed back that i was the best daughter anyone could ever have. I turned around for a second and then saw the most saddest think a daughter could see. My father was being beaten. Blood poured out of his chest as the knife came out. I stared for a second and then something clicked inside of me. I grabbed the nearest object and plunged it through him. After she had shown toni her flashback tears started to fill her eyes. What happened next?, toni asked.

What happened next was the worst part

of it all. The leader whispered something to the second leader. She came over and grabbed me by the hair and started to drag me away. I screamed for my father. She put me onto one of the shuttles with no food or water and sent me off. I cried and screamed for hours. I knew that i would never see my father ever again.

I saw a huge rock coming towards me. I tried to control the shuttle but it t wasn't working. I started kicking a door but nothing happened. The last thing remember was waking up here and seeing the women.

Chapter 12

Frenemies?

Location: Planet X

Time: Unknown

And there she stood, confused and scared.
Poppie didn't know what or who she was,
she appeared out of nowhere. What was

she doing here? Is she here to harm Poppie
or her family? She began to walk further
towards her, she didn't know what to do,
she stood shaking not knowing whether
these few minutes could possibly be the
last few minutes of her life! The closer she
got the more she panicked and she knew
she only had one decision, it was a life or
death situation (at least that's what she
thought,) and she wasn't prepared to die.

She quickly pulled out her gun, aimed
it at the creature and got ready to fire, and
suddenly this creature put her hands in the
air. She wasn't here to harm Poppie, she
was in trouble and needed help, she had
cuts and bruises all over her. She had a
silver shimmering body that reflected the
sunlight, with vibrant pink hair and blue
sparkling eyebrows. Once Poppie knew

she wasn't going to cause trouble, she lowered her gun and put it too the floor then gave her a signal to show her it was safe to come over, she hobbled closer and introduced herself, her name was Crypton. Before Poppie had the chance to introduce herself, she began to speak in a soft, delicate, squeaky voice.

She explained that she had been kicked out of the alien army because she had asked the Alien leader not to fight as she thought it was unnecessary. She didn't believe that fighting was the answer, so she was punished for this and The Alien leader, not only kicked her out, but then injured her face. She then said that she wasn't going to fight for the alien leader as she was punished for standing up for what she believed in. The Alien leader made her scared and frightened of what may happen if she went back, so she decided not too so that she could avoid any other punishments he may be waiting to give her. She then began to ask Poppie what she was doing here as fighting was only for men and she was a women.

Poppie joined the army as a man, as it was something she really wanted to do so that she could stay fit and healthy, she was always willing to do as much as she could to keep her body in good shape and make sure she was eating a healthy balanced diet and joining the army was just another way for her to do it, whilst also doing what she enjoys. Not only did she join because she wanted to stay healthy, it was also because she was a previous gang member and she began to realise that constantly getting into trouble with the police and making innocent people feel uncomfortable, wasn't the right life for her. Being sat outside doing nothing all day wasn't something she enjoyed, and it certainly wasn't a way of staying healthy, if anything she was going in totally the wrong direction, not just in ways of staying healthy, but also ways of what people think about her, and she was putting herself on a lower level than what she was actually capable off, so she decided to change that.

Poppie believed that all women should be able to do what men can do, as they are all equal.She wasn't going to give up on what she believed in, that's not the person she was. She knew that if anyone found out she would get in serious trouble however, she still went ahead.Poppie was a happy person, until it come to people being treated differently or people expect more of them because of their gender, because both men and women are capable to do the same, which is why she took the risk of joining the army and faking her identity. Growing up, Poppie had a strong relationship with her brother, Tony, which sometimes caused problems when he was able to do things that she wasn't because of their genders. Poppie and Tony not being able to do some things together is just another reason she thinks men and women should be treated equally.

Chapter 13

Revenge Is Sweet

Location: Planet X

Time: Unknown

The alien told her why she was kicked off the ship and that the alien leader is going to start a war. She began to get her troops ready for battle. All the children gathered around and prayed that everything will be ok. At first everyone was scared of the alien outcast but once they heard her story they became friends. Poppie walked away without telling anyone where she was going. Crypton, the outcast alien, discretely ran after her. She finally found her sat alone crying.

"We won't win" she said Quickly. She told Crypton all about her experiences with the aliens, How tortured her father into leaving . "What if you had a alien on your team?" Crypton hinted.

The soldier had a glimpse of light in her eye which the alien had never seen before. Then it faded. She explained to her that the human leader would never approve of an alien working with them. Crypton was

confused at why he wouldn't let her join.
His daughter was taken a few years ago.
He hasn't been the same since.

"Take me to him", Crypton demanded.
As poppie opened the door the human dropped
his luggage. He was scared at first but
then he calmed down.

"Why is she here, get her out of here"
he said.

"I want to join your army", Crypton
shouted. He stood up and laughed in her
face. "I know about your daughter" she
said. His face dropped as he sat down. I
can get her back. His face lifted and she
could see the relief in his eyes. Crypton
told him about the scheming plan for war.
"If you let me join your group I can help
you get your daughter back. If we win the
war I can get her back" crypton bargained.

He wiped a tear from his face and agreed.

We should plan ahead so they don't see us coming.He finished wiping his tears away as we made the plan. The aliens weakest point is death if we kill enough of their men they might back down. They don't like living in greive. Crypton explained that she can sneak onto the ship and have a look around maybe the child will be in there. How old will she be now? Crypton asked.. He looked at me blankly.

She was wearing a pink dress when she was taken. The leader changed the subject quickly. Crypton started to work out a battle routine of who goes to the front and how they will get the child out. "I will sneak onto the ship and find her she might be scared at first but I will tell her that you're here.You will finally see your daughter again!" I encouraged.

She was sat viewing the river. "It's lovely" Crypton said. She explained that she would come here with her dad when she was little and sing songs with him. Crypton told her that she was going to find the leader's daughter. "What if they killed her?" poppie said. Crypton said that the aliens weren't capable of killing a child but then she thought to herself that she has never seen a Human child on the ship. Had Crypton gave the human leader false hope.

Chapter 14

Double-Crossed

Location: Zurg City

Time: Unknown

"MAKE SURE YOU DO IT RIGHT THIS TIME" screamed the vile alien leader (A.L.) . L.U.N.A, the second in command walked in . "Good morning master, what has the worthless little thing done now?" she asked tensely, hoping for her life that the aliens leaders poisonous slimy tentacles wouldn't somehow slither around her neck. "Nothing, just breathing however I may have too put an end too that soon ." he stalked over to the metallic slanted wall .He held his tentacle against it and it flashed open inside was the most glamorous range of weapons ever how I would love to get my hands on one of those weapons one day thought L.U.N.A wistfully . A.L. turned around his tentacles slowly growing more and more venomous, " WHAT DID YOU SAY ?" roared the A.L. L.U.N.A. slowly took a step back . Cowering she replied " N...nothing my master, I said nothing . " She looked anywhere but at her master, hoping that her master was not reading her mind.

"HOW COULD YOU AFTER ALL THIS TIME YOU HAVE BEEN PLOTTING AGAINST ME!"

"Plotting against YOU! There's no need to do that considering the way you run this place!"

" YOU, I'M GOING TO KILL YOU, GET BACK HERE . NOW" he bellowed after the second in command . There was a deafening bang and a fire erupted from nowhere.   Running for her life L.U.N.A had only one thought in her head I need to find the outcasts father . The gleamy walls were shaking so intently that it would be a miracle if they survived, the A.L. was screaming and his tentacles where like a tornado killing anything in it's path . L.U.N.A

95

was scanning her eyes through the smoke hoping to find the emergency exit . Finally, after what felt to her like a year she saw it and in an attempt to miss the poison tentacles trying to find her neck she made a dive for the door.

The fresh air hit her and she started to walk along planet X Where would an outcasts parent hide ? she thought desperately . After walking a mile east it hit her, he would go somewhere quiet where no one could look at him as a disgrace to their kind. Two days she traveled to get to the rugged mountains, knowing it would be too risky to board my 8000000 mile per hour ship, when she arrived it was like a whole new world . The once destroyed mountains where now replaced by buildings that could withstand up to a level

6 attack and even the floor was a strong metal probably chromium she thought.

"May I help you?" said the calming yet strict voice of the outcasts father- Kwayzar

.

L.U.N.A. no clue how to do this so she started explaining everything, she felt strange speaking to Kwayzar (especially considering the fact that she said they should make his son an outcast). However, he listened and after explaining everything from when she realised that the A.L. was bad news, he merely said " I see " . L.U.N.A just stared she had no clue what would happen next so he said softly, " You believe you have been witless and wish to make amends. We all make mistakes what matters however is what you can do to fix them ." He looked into her eyes and she thought

" Kwayzar i can get you in the A.L. is HQ but i will not be able to promise anyone who goes in there alive will come out alive. I know the coordinates and all the defences he has there ." She looked at him and he her "Let's do it . I will organise a meeting now this will be a volunteer mission only. "

" Servant! HERE NOW!" Shrieked the A.L., a younger alien with deep purple skin and silver misty eyes. "Boy I need you to find out what is going on, the little rat has disappeared of the planet and could be plotting with rebels against me ." The servant looked shocked, clearly he thought that the idea of rebellion was a miracle but luckily the A.L. had other things on his mind so he muttered " Yes master " and of he went . The only thought on the A.L.

mind was "What is going on ?" . After a while he just couldn't stand it so he went to the room full of his best technology.

The moment he entered those brave enough to talk fell silent as if a button was pushed. The servant was stood in front of the defences reprogramming it, "WHAT ARE YOU DOING ?" he roared . The alien boy dropped the keyboard out of shock,

" There coming, there on the way. I was just making the defences stronger we all are making sure they are at the strongest point so our master is safe ." he wildly made up everyone nodded in agreement. " I must go to the emergency bunker has anyone prepared that ? " he glared at them all. "Yes I will show you to it now Master." replied a brave alien.

As he left the aliens slowly walked around

checking all the defences went from 500 to 1000 . Meanwhile in the bunker A.L. was speaking more to himself than anyone else, "They must be coming to kill me why else would they be here, I mean they must realise that they can't just come and be my slaves ." The servant that had shown him to his bunker was barely listening he was loosening the doors so they were to seen by the rebels . "WHY ARE YOU OPENING THE DOORS ?"

A.L. was looking like he would explode his tentacles where slithering along the floor and things where catching fire . All through the building the aliens were getting emergency supplies and shutting down all the emergency space shuttles . A blanket of smoke was covering the smoke as the alien who escorted the A.L. came sprinting in "

HE KNOWS! HE KNOWS! LOCK THE BUNKER, HE KNOWS!" he screamed . Suddenly the doors burst open and in came the rebels.

Seeing the state of the control room and how all the defences had been lowered the rebels lowered their weapons and just stared . After a few minutes a crash was heard from below and Kwayzar was suddenly back to head rebel mode. " Right, listen up, we don't have long so it's better we do this quick those of you who wish to join the rebels and fight over here . Then those who have been injured or kept prisoner to the left." The aliens separated into two groups and then Kwayzar shouted again " Planet X is an alien planet as you know there are humans here and we rebels believe in an equal world between the two if you disagree and wish to fight then you may if not you will either stay or go to safety." The injured were lead out for the first time in years and the others were handed weapons. " We locked him in an emergency bunker pretending that it was for his safety it's on fire down there but he can see in fire your best chance is smoke.

"SMOKE BOMBS AT THE READY, THREE TWO NOW!" the doors burst open and the A.L. attacked at the same time . Realising that there was no way he could fight them all, he decided that his best hope was to escape to his secret army and start a war . As he got to the exit a searing white hot pain shot through a tentacle then it was gone and so was he.

Chapter 15

The Uprising

Location: Planet X

Time: Unknown

"I have had my daughter taken away from me. Due to what? You may ask. She was exiled for anti-war views. Essentially, she was exiled for thought crime." Kwayzar Xor Zkuwol exclaimed, a large crowd interested viewers and media representatives following him, background smalltalk filling the moments in between his statements. Police also seemed interested, despite multiple attempts to "discipline" Xor for disagreeing police and citizens. He had a march of about 2000 people supporting him. The intimidating force eventually fell into violence against those who strongly disagreed with their points. Eventually, Xor's more zealotous followers ended up violently rebelling.

After a while, the police could no longer take the pressure, and the army was called in. The army struggled to contain the protesters, who had now armed themselves. Some army and police allied with Xor's cause, and starting wreaking mass havoc upon the army and law enforcement. Shortly after, the area was in anarchy.

"OOH-RAH! OOH-RAH! OOOHHH-RAAAHHHH!!" The massive crowd of armed rebels overwhelmed and crushed all resistance in their path uncontrollably, Xor was positioned at the very front of the crowd, commanding his force and moralizing them. The cramped urban space provided an easy environment for the rebels to take control of. The rebels kept growing in numbers until they became a tsunami, sweeping through the narrow, old streets, and their numbers only got stronger when they did – many police and military shared the same view as Xor, but did not have the courage to stand up to those who didn't. For them, this was liberation.

After 2 tumultuous days of fighting with high losses on both sides, the rebels found themselves stuck on the road to the capital, the government military was held up in makeshift barricades along and on the road, and no matter how many soldiers the rebels sent, they would always hold them off. By this point, pro-government militias were harassing the rebels using guerilla tactics, preventing them from moving a large enough force to flank the fortifications. Xor chose to go to a government building in one of the major cities his followers had captured and broadcast his orders from there rather than be shot dead by some militia.

However, more than 5000 miles away, in an old, rusted outbuilding of a human military base, 3 people were attempting to operate a machine, the machine ran through all of the inner perimeter of the outbuilding, bar a small area for the exit door, however the machine was surprisingly pristine, unlike the building that housed it. It was rather simple despite its size, and was almost silent.

"Aye, what's this?" asked one of the men at the back of the formation, his thick Scottish accent echoing through the room.

"This, is a mass radio listener. Invented only recently, it was designed for espionage, and to intercept enemy communications, you will use it to find the frequency, or frequencies, the alien radios operate on, " the man at the front of the formation told him, the person next to the Scottish man seemed to already know, perhaps he was better at espionage than anyone else thought. He droned on about how to use it for hours, boring his comrades.

"So, now that you know, get to work!" he commanded.

The Scottish man seemed to have listened for a longer time than he did, and proceeded to flick a few switches and press some buttons, before entering a frequency range and sample time onto a computer, which looked like an old ATM machine.

"Ah, there we go." he sighed.

A series of white noise with gradually higher pitch played, increasing the frequency and pitch every 10 seconds, until they began to hear a strange noise, which sounded like the aliens they were waging war with, however they heard something odd, it seemed to be a radio not broadcast from the alien capital, and also seemed to broadcast antigovernment statements,

"D'ya think someone's started a resistance'?" asked the Scottish man

"Definitely, doubt it's a trap, you can hear nothing from the background, and our radio receivers occasionally receive military transmissions from someplace in the capital if they were on the wrong frequency, " replied his companion.

"We got broadcast equipment?"

"Should do."

He pressed a button to stay on the frequency the transmitter was on.

The companion opened a thin cupboard which held a slightly dusty radio transmitter, he proceeded to wipe the dust off and placed it on the floor, then picked up a microphone from a shelf on the wall, and connected it to the transmitter. He cleared his throat and exclaimed

"Is this a frequency on which rebels against our opposing state communicate?"

"Yes. Would you be willing to aid our cause in exchange for future support?"

"I would first have to ask my superiors, but what do you intend?"

"We wish for material and military aid against our foes, direct or indirect, I also wish to identify myself. My name is Kwazar Xor Zkuwol."

"It's done, it should be here soon, stand by for now, " the Scottish man said. He and his companion walked out the outbuilding to a dark night sky.

"God help them." The Scotsman whispered.

Chapter 16

A flash of My Life

Location: Planet X

Time: Unknown

It all happened so quickly, Poppie's life

flashed before her eyes. Growing up, in my family home where I lived with my Mum, Dad and Brother. I was very happy and confident I always used to play games with my brother Tony, we were best friends, however we were sadly separated when we were young due to our parents splitting up. After that I spent the rest of my childhood growing up with my mother in the same family home we always lived in. Losing my brother and my father at such a young age caused many problems growing up, I went from being a bubbly kid to being quiet and dull which then lead me to join gangs at the age of 14, which sent me in the completely wrong direction. I used to spend my days sat on benches in parks till late at night, making locals feel intimidated, whilst drinking and smoking and I always got into trouble with the police. At the time I didn't think much of this, until a few months ago when I realised that what I was doing was wrong and I needed to stop, I decided I wanted to join the army.'

Once I joined the army, my life began to fall back into place. I was doing something I had always wanted to do, I was happier than I had been in many years. I made new friends who were also in the army with me, even though they were all males we got on well and it felt like after all these years I had someone to talk too. I also started to gain a relationship with my brother again, as he was also in the army and it was the same as it had always been, we sat together laughing and joking every chance that we got, even if it wasn't meant to be funny we would always find a way, that was just the sense of humour we had.

3

Now everything I had is going to get taken away from me, just because I stood up for what I believed in and followed my heart. I can't even say I regret what I did, I knew there was going to be consequences if anyone found out, and that didn't stop me. I'm proud that I did what I did, even though it did come to this. I knew that if anything bad was to come from this that I would be an inspiration to many people and hopefully encourage people to also, go ahead and follow their heart, and stand up for what they believe in even if it's not what other people think is right.

Chapter 17

Identified and Executed

Location: Planet X

Time: Unknown

As Poppie went into the female lavatory, she was caught off guard and before she had the chance to explain she had mistaken it for the male lavatory, who she really was had been identified and her secret was out. She begged and begged for him to keep it a secret, she promised she would do anything he asked of her but the male soldier who had caught her went straight to the human leader, and Poppie was called into the leader's office. She was then told that due to the fact she had lied about who she was in such serious conditions that were war, she would have to face the consequences of execution.Poppie didn't know what to do, this was the fear she had been waiting for, she wasn't ready to lose her brother nor her friends. She began to kick and scream, hoping that the human leader would change his mind on this dreadful consequence. However this made matters worse and Poppie ended up in more bother than she previously was.

The human leader demanded Poppie to a field in the middle of nowhere, he lay her down on a raised wooden board in the centre of the grass, and pulled out a large, deadly axe. Poppie lay there shaking in fear, she was crying and begging the leader not to go through with the execution. However she had no choice, she was going to die. He swung the axe viciously towards her throat and as it plunged through her, blood chaotically came firing out. The crowd cheered as the so called male who betrayed them was no longer part of their lives and they could now fight and win the battle against the Aliens. However Tony fell to the floor as his heart had shattered into a million tiny pieces, the only good memory he had as a child had been destroyed and there was nothing he could have done about it. Tony slowly wandered back home, his head was full of questions; Could i have helped Poppie escape? If i stood up for her, would she still here? Is it my fault she was executed?

After the death of his sister, Tony didn't do much for a few days, he sat in one room thinking everything that happened was his fault. He didn't eat, he barely drank and he stayed in the same, dirty, sweaty clothes for days on end. Losing his sister had broke him, especially in such a tragic way, but a few days he finally started to become back to his normal self. Tony never forgot about this event and he never will, it'll live with him forever.

Chapter 18

The Break-In

Location: Indigo City, Planet X

Time: Unknown

The aliens had arrived outside of the human's city, it was very clear that the humans had advanced since the first time they had met because the alien leader could sense a strong force that was surrounding the city. A.L. stared at the city, it was very clear that he had wanted to do more than just attack the humans but destroy their city. After a while of standing in silence the alien leader turned to the troops and ordered them to attack the humans. The soldiers went forward until they were standing in front of the alien leader they began to run towards the city until they stopped. The aliens looked confused until they realised what was stopping them from going into the city.

The aliens were staring at the forcefield which was surrounding the human's, city it seems like they were prepared for an attack. The forcefield acted as a barrier to stop all other species except the humans from getting through. "It was a good attempt to keep unwanted visitors out however the humans did not think about the fact that my kind have access to advanced technology." thought the alien leader. Although they also have advanced technology the humans had not been on this planet for long so the humans wouldn't know how to use the full power of a forcefield.

At first the alien leader was surprised that the humans would be so advanced to have a technology such as force fields especially when they hadn't been on this planet for a long period of time. The fact that they have access to this technology didn't really affect A.L. plan. However she was sure can speak for all of the aliens and say that they hadn't expect that from the humans.

Even Though the forcefield only allowed humans to get through to the city the soldiers continued to try and destroy the forcefield. A.L. just stand on the sidelines watching his soldiers continue to attack the force field with no luck. After minutes of waiting A.L. finally stepped forward and was clearly very tired of waiting around for his soldiers to destroy the forcefield.

After waiting for the soldiers to obey A.L.'s orders and destroy the forcefield it seemed like A.L. had finally grown impatient with her soldiers who were incapable of breaking through a simple force field. A.L. walked in front of the soldiers who were tired and very clearly wanted to give up. A.L. was finally going to show the rest of his kind the power that he had been hiding from them all. Since A.L. usually made his servants do all the work while he just watched from the side it is a rare opportunity to see A.L. do any work.

As A.L. walked up to the forcefield the aliens could see the look of dread on the soldiers' faces they seemed to think that A.L. was going to harm them however he just walked past them. It wasn't surprising that the A.L. didn't harm the soldiers, if he did that it would be harmful to his plan. A.L. walked until he was right in front of the force field the aliens knew that the forcefield wasn't very powerful but didn't know how weak it actually was. A.L. touched the forcefield with her finger and all of a sudden the whole force field shattered.

The force field that was once surrounding the city shattered into millions of tiny pieces. The A.L. shouting orders at the soldiers who were staring at the display in front of them in amazement. Of course as soon as the first obstacle was eliminated he would go back to barking orders like he always did, I wasn't surprised at all it was always like this however the soldiers were clearly still distracted. I stood back and watched the troops, they entered the human's city and began to follow A.L.'s order.

Chapter 19

The Battle

Location: Indigo City, Planet X

Time: Unknown

Suddenly, the aliens arrived at the force-field dome and aggressively started to attack it. The aliens were not giving up on trying to break the force field dome. The dome was slowly beginning to crack and the aliens began to prepare for battle with the humans. The humans began to panic as the dome was cracking all over and slowly falling to pieces.

The air was filled with crying screams as the dome force field shattered and the battle finally begun. The aliens viciously started to attack the humans with more force and they slowly began to lose. There was no going back for the humans now. You could see the frustration on the Human Leaders face as his team began to lose the battle.He was trying everything he could too push his team and make them more confident but nothing was working for them. The Human Leader was now giving up on hope that his team was going to win the battle.

The humans are now beginning to lose the battle more, howeverthe outcast alien had a plan for the humans. But then, the alien outcast asked Tom if she could she join their team. Tom was confused at this moment but then began to understand why she wanted to switch teams. Tony agreed to let Crypton join their team to try and win the battle.

As the humans began to pick up their pace again the aliens slowly began to die and orange sparkly blood squirted all over Planet X and created holes in the floor because their blood was acidic.The

More aliens that die, the more holes that are created in the floor.

More rebel aliens started to arrive and the A.L. (alien leader) started to spurt

127

her tentacles and chop them in half. Alien body parts were flying everywhere over the battlefield. The alien leader was now killing hundreds of aliens at a time.

All of the alien soldiers were changing sides and trying to kill the rest of the aliens that are left to help the humans win the blatte. The aliens were fighting against their own kind because they're to weak too try and win against the humans.

As the battle dragged on the A.L. began to shoot deep purple ropes to catch their enemy this binds them and puts them into a deep sleep. This gives the humans less aliens to kill so that they will win the battle first. This also means that the aliens will have a harder chance a trying to win the battle.

This would be remembered as the most

violent and tragic battle in history if anyone survived. A loud bang shook the planet
and L.U.N.A. was blasted back of her feet
just as a tentacle had almost reached her
neck.   he shouldn't of sent that explo-
sion should you   thought L.U.N.A. as she
rushed back into battle. Over on the other
side Kwayzar was battling endlessly with
alien after alien after alien.

The battle was ferocious, nowhere in
the battlefield was safe, as more holes burned
in the planet causing innocent people to
fall into the holes it was realised by the
rebel aliens that they had to be taken to
safety. A new plan was made "if it worked
great if not there would be no humans left"
thought Kwayzar apprehensively .   The
fastest aliens gathered up the last living
humans and a small group of aliens who

could be spared lead them safely to a rebel bunker until the battle ceased.

Blood, blood was everywhere, in the air, on the floor it seemed nowhere was not covered in blood. As aliens, rebel or not, battled for what they believed was the right way to run the planet. No one was safe and no one was sorry for what they had done. Dead bodies were lying everywhere and where a major tripping hazard if you needed to run forward and take someone's place in battle. The alien leader was now slicing people in half or strangling people using her deadly tentacles.

Chapter 20

The Savior

```
Location: Indigo City,  Planet X

Time: Unknown
```

The bloodthirsty battle was still happening and the aliens were winning. They were getting stronger and the outcast alien needed to leave to find the child of the human leader. Throughout the battle she was thinking that the child might be dead and that she may have given him false hope.The stench of blood fills the air as many people were being slaughtered. The alien was running out of things to do, to win and the soldiers were giving up. As Crypton looked across the battlefield he saw a glimpse of pink run across the field. Could this be the humans leaaders daughter? Crypton had to make an important decision should she save the daughter or help fight the aliens.

Crypton ran across the field dodging any bullets she could. As she quietly looked in every ship she finally found her. She had blue eyes and long golden hair. She was wearing a pink dress as her father said she

would. As Crypton walked towards her
she backed away but then Crypton told
her about her father and she hugged crypton and started to cry. As they walked
across the field she ran towards her father.
Tears in both of there eyes. "You saved
her" he said

The humans and rebel aliens are slowly
beginning to defeat more aliens and are
getting closer to the alien leader. As the
aliens fell Tony picked up one of their silver weapons and not knowing what would
happen pulled the trigger . An estimate
of fifty aliens were set on fire and disinte-
grated into ashes.

As the battle burned on Tony found the
alien's weapon pretty useful. All through
the battle field aliens were falling.

Tony turned to see a hideous alien aim-

ing his blaster at him surrounded by people fighting, Tony had no choice but to
come to terms with the fact that this was
his end. As the alien took his final aim,
a great silver flash and nothing more was
left of his best friend, who was now unless
his senses were lying dead on the floor just
five metres away.

" CRYPTON! NO! " cried Tony as the
humans were bought back. He ran forward
through the battle and the alien rebels stop
wondering what is going on, " Don't be
dead, please, don't be dead ." he was shouting now as if the louder he were the more
chance he would have at being alive. His
hands reached his neck and by instinct checked
for a pulse. When there was none he burst
into tears and the human leader started to
lead him away.

There was a sudden commotion in the alien leaders army the rebels turned ready to attack but what they saw was completely breathtaking. Most of the A.L. soldiers were lying their weapons on the ground completely refusing to fight ore where turning to face the last of alien leaders army.

Twenty meters away from Tony there was a low grumbling noise that broke the deafening silence. Everyone just stared mystified when a boys strangled scream was heard " Crypton! YOU'RE ALIVE, YOU'RE ALIVE!" he broke free of the human leaders grip and ran towards his new best friend to hug him. " Stop strangling me or I'll be dead again." Crypton said hoarsely. A sudden movement in the A.L. army and then the alien leader shouted " ANNIHILATE THEM ALL!"

The last of the alien leaders army who had stayed to fight bravely charged forward and Crypton filled with a burning rage charged forward and finished them all of single handedly .Then, when the only alien left in the alien leaders army was the alien leader...

" I think you are forgetting me!" pronounced the alien leader harshly. Every head turned to face her and every head had an utter look of disgust upon its face whether it was human or alien." ARE YOU WILLING TO FIGHT EVERYONE HERE!" screamed an outraged Tony. "No, not fight but I will destroy you all."

Chapter 21

Rebelled

Location: Indigo City, Planet X

Time: Unknown

The second in command stood and stared at the scene in front of her because of her kind's foolishness one of their own had died

to save someone that they were against.
If this didn't prove to A.L. fighting the
humans was not the right way L.U.N.A
didn't know what would because the death
would be on his hands. He was the one at
fault he was the one who encouraged his
kind to go to war with the humans, he was
the one who wanted to go to war with the
humans. It was hard for L.U.N.A to understand why this had happened. What
was there to gain from starting a war?

This all happened because of A.L., he
was the one who had started this and L.U.N.A
would yet again be the one to fix the mess
he had created. Usually she would not
fight because she didn't think that she was
required to but somebody needed to put
an end to the war. L.U.N.A did not intend
to kill A.L. because he was much stronger

than her however she would be able to distract A.L. so the rebellion could attack. She didn't believe that she could defeat him there is a reason she was only second in command but she was sure the rebellion would have a chance.

A.L. had been expecting at least one of his kind to rebel against him during the war, as he was aware of the hatred most of the aliens had towards him and his ideas. He definitely knew that his second in command didn't agree with the war from the start, she never fought alongside him and his soldiers because she didn't wish to be a part of the war there was no doubt in her mind that he had noticed. The whole time L.U.N.A had been dodging attacks from A.L. she knew none of her attacks would be effective against the alien leader. She was about to get hit by an attack when the rebellion group had appeared, they had a better chance of defeating A.L. than L.U.N.A did. Although she was second in command she was still only a teenager and she didn't enjoy fighting, she thought it was mostly a waste of her time.

Finally the rebellion against A.L. had arrived and it appeared like they seeked revenge. L.U.N.A recognised the leader of the rebellion to be the father of the outcast who had died only minutes before. His facial expression did not show anger nor did it show rage it didn't even seem display sorrow, it was clear to L.U.N.A that he didn't know what to feel after witnessing the death of his daughter. Usually the situation at hand would leave one distraught and unable to express their feelings of despair after losing someone so close and dear to them. As it would appear the leader of the rebellion would have to be able to control his feelings and not show any weakness to the enemy.

L.U.N.A was relieved that the rebellion against the alien leader had arrived when they did to help defeat him because she knew that if A.L. wasn't defeated then the war would continue until no one was left to fight. In reality the war was started just for the alien leaders entertainment. In the end so many innocent lives were lost for entertainment purposes, the war had no meaning. The leader of the rebellion had seemed to come to his senses and realized what was going on. His daughter had just died and because of this he and the rest of

141

the rebellion group had picked a fight with the leader of his kind.

After the rest of the aliens who remained alive had seen their leader kill one of his own they lost all the respect that they had once had for their leader. They had seen A.L. for what he really was and they were not pleased about what the had discovered. They realised that the war was only started because their leader was bored and wanted some excitement in his life. This caused the rest of the aliens to attack their leader who had lied to them and treated them like slaves for years. They wanted their revenge for being treated like slaves and they were going to get it.

The rest of the aliens who were once part of A.L.'s troops turned on their leader and joined the rebellion to defeat their leader.

All of the aliens had betrayed their leader however they still found it difficult to defeat him. What happened next was not only a shock to the rebellion but the alien leader also, it was thought to be impossible. The alien who was thought to be dead was standing once again.

After the outcast alien stood up she started to walk toward the members of the rebellion with a small smile. While everyone was stood still in shock the alien continued walking until she was standing in front of the traumatized alien leader. Before the alien leader could say anything the outcast alien punched him in the stomach sending him to the ground with a grunt of pain. As the alien leader attempted to stand up he was kicked across the floor by the outcast alien. The outcast had somehow been able to send the leader of aliens to the ground and continued to attack him.

The outcast continued to attack the alien leader without allowing him to speak or attack back. Although the leader was on the ground and unable to get back up it wasn't possible for the outcast to defeat the alien leader by kicking and punching him. Suddenly the outcast pulled out a knife that had been hiding in his pocket since he had first visited Tony's house. The outcast then stabbed the alien leader in the back with the knife before turning around to face the rest of the aliens who were watching in surprise at how the outcast was able to eliminate the alien leader.

After the alien leader was eliminated Tony walks over to the outcast alien holding out one of his hands. One by one the humans walked over to the aliens and held out their hands as an offering of peace however this time the peace offering was accepted. Both the aliens and the humans finally realised that they didn't have to fight each other.

Chapter 22

Our Mutual Friends

Location: Indigo City, Planet X

Time: Unknown

"Be seated, " Thomas stated. His grayscale

suit and tie outfit made him indistinguish-
able from his peers behind him. The alien
ambassador obeyed, and Thomas followed
suite. The cold, red leather seats match-
ing the clean, opaque gloss roundtable provided a pleasant aesthetic to the area. The
ambassador and Thomas Oswald awkwardly
stared at each other blankly.

"So, " started Thomas,

"We are glad to hear of the at least tem-
porary peace between our two nations, "
he added.

"We are also pleased to hear of this, "
replied the alien ambassador.

"Due to this, we believe it is optimal,
and in both of our nation's best interests to
begin "We agree with your interpretation
of the status quo."

The alien ambassador and Thomas chatted for what must've been hours, but soon enough negotiations were about to be over

"So we shall return to the status quo?" asked Thomas

"Ultimately, we believe it is in our best interests to return unconditional peace to our world, " replied the Alien ambassador

"So that therefore concludes our negotiation with status quo ante bellum, correct?" Thomas questioned.

"Indeed, " clarified the ambassador.

The company of both the ambassador and leader applauded.

"We are greatly pleased with this diplomatic settling, " Thomas exclaimed. Suddenly, cameramen burst into the room to interview Oswald, meanwhile the ambassador walked out to a strange alien aircraft, and flew off into the light-green sky.

Peace had returned, and it would be everlasting.

The room was loud and echoing with a bustling rebel population. The alien diplomat glared at them all, but discovered that Xor, the leader had watched him do so.

"Don't be insolent, Mr. Rxyl." Xor told him. "Very rowdy these lot, but they are not to be toiled with, " Xor added. Rxyl took a seat on the rickety, wooden chair, defaced with rebellion doctrine, with Xor and his guards on the opposite side, sitting in an ornate orange chair.

"Silence, my brothers and sisters!" Xor yelled as politely as possible.

"We must not let war define who we are as people, " Xor added. "Now, let us negotiate beneficial peace." Xor asked.

"As you would expect, Mr. Zkuwol, we

are confident that we know your motives behind the war you have waged against us – particularly our leader."

"It is not particularly your leader I have chose to wage war against, the civil and military doctrine you follow is much too strict. For example, the death penalty for refusing to follow orders. I fear this type of doctrine will lead to a detrimental loss of soldiers who merely were mistook – and that my life would fall to this. It was also the incompetency of our leaders which ultimately caused me to rise up along with my comrades, and form my own fair state. If you refuse to grant us our own state, with recognition, and out of your lands, please leave now, " spoke Xor Zkuwol.

Rxyl had to make a huge decision, either lose a large amount of land for his country, or continue a bloodshed that his people yearned to stop. Before he could make an actual decision, Xor started.

"So, you will allow us our own state?"

Rxyl knew that Xor was trying to play mind games with him – and succeeding. Rxyl could simply not resist the pressure and intimidation caused by the massive army behind him, Rxyl began to grow nervous.

"I'll ask you again, will you allow us our own recognised, sovereign state out of your territory?"

Xor asked, seeming even more angered and intimidating this time.

"Ahh uhh ugh, sorry, yes, we will allow you and those currently in your zone of control a recognised, sovereign state unconditionally should our negotiations succeed." fluttered Rxyl, breaking the deathly silence that hung over the room for some time.

"That is all we want, thank you for your time." Xor concluded. Without warning, the immense crowd behind him burst into a deafening chant.

"OOH-RAH OOH-RAH OOOOH-RAAAAAAHHH!!"

A massive flare of bullets and explosions went off through the mud and air, it was a hectic, confusing, stagnant battle-field, thousands of lives on both sides was getting nobody anywhere, you'd occasionally hear news radio stations flare through one side which would blubber about all the violence and war of the current day. But then suddenly, 2 massive shouts to cease fire were heard, they travelled a seemingly near-infinite distance, echoing eternally through

153

the empty space. Suddenly, silence fell. People stopped dead in their tracks, all that could be heard was "Cease fire, my dear friends, this war is no longer, you can go home." Unexpectedly, there wasn't a chant, or cheer. People just rested there. The war had consumed them as people, and they were a shadow of their former selves. They had lost many friends and family all to a diplomatic mishap. Innocent people were killed, all for practically nothing.

THE END

Printed in Great Britain
by Amazon